Frappe
Scones
And
The
Boy I love

DEONDRE MARCELLO

DEDICATION

To my best friends that told me to believe in myself
and for my friends that are still searching for love,
hold on, our time is coming.

"No one has imagined us. We want to live like trees, sycamores blazing through the sulfuric air, dappled with scars, still exuberantly budding, our animal passion rooted in the city."

– *Adrienne Rich*

CH. 1

My day started off normal, I prepared my breakfast and did my tedious morning workouts. I'm slightly obsessed with having a lean body, yet I eat like a pig most days. Whatever work I did was immediately canceled out. To be honest, it may just be my own insecurities, I always feel like I'm less attractive because I don't have the type of body you see in the movies or those guys at the gym have.

I shook my head and reminded myself that I am more than enough and that I am perfectly imperfect just the way I am. This was my mantra whenever intrusive thoughts or self-doubt came creeping in. Over the years I got to saying morning affirmations and found that they helped me on a subconscious level.

Anyway, I'd usually cool off, take a shower and then play video games for a while to take my mind away from things further before I truly got my day started. Today however was different, I was meeting my friend Ethan for a little hangout. It's not every day we get to hangout like we usually do because his work normally took him out of state a lot for different periods of time, but April was just about finished, and his contract was up so May was the beginning of us hanging out a lot more. I'm super excited because Ethan was the one guy I had grown to appreciate in my life. We had grown close over the past couple of years, a lot faster than most people I'd let into my life and pretty much bonded on a level that was surreal to me. To me, Ethan was everything a guy should be, and he was all the man I'd ever dreamed of.

Sounds perfect but unfortunately life isn't a fairy tale, at least mine wasn't and there was a slight problem that kept it from being a story of legends. Ethan was completely straight, and this was infuriating. This wasn't because he was a regular, everyday heterosexual but because I couldn't bring myself to tell Ethan that I liked guys and that I might love him. Who am I kidding? I do love him and although I've hinted at my few interactions with those of the same gender, he's never asked me about it, nor has he ever made any advances for that matter.

Nevertheless, I value our friendship and I honestly feel like jeopardizing that would hurt too much. I'm thinking too much, I said to myself. I took a nice long shower to cool off and focus, then I took out one of my silk shirts. I rarely dress up, but I figured that I had to look my best, after all it's not every day we get to spend time together and it's been so long, it couldn't hurt to dress a little nicer.

We were meant to meet up for ten o'clock and it was now twenty minutes to the hour. I finished grooming and prepping myself and was now ready. The ride into the city was a short one as I lived close to the city outskirts. I got out my phone and gave Ethan a nudge, letting him know that I was already there. I waited awhile and realized that the message was sent but not received. Just one tick, so I figured he probably doesn't have service. I could give him a call, but I didn't mind killing some time, so I took a small walk to a bar and had about two beers until my phone rang fifteen minutes later.

I answered, "Hello?" "Hey bro"

"Hey Ethan, I dropped you a message but no response, where are you?"

"Oh yeah, I forgot to renew my plan man, total snooze but I'm in the city, so meet at the regular spot?"

"Stalemates Coffee Corner, you got it, see you in fifteen then"

"Great, catch you in a few then" he said and hung up.

I quickly finished my remaining beer, cleared my tab and left a generous tip to the bartender who looked at me with such a shock that I simply smiled and said have a good day.

I know what the industry is like, I've worked several odd jobs in hospitality before and sometimes a random act of kindness or in this case, a nice tip is more than enough to get your spirits up and hopeful for better days.

Now I briskly took off in the direction of Stalemate's, excited to meet my best pal. It was the start of a lifetime of excitement, adventures and memories I would cherish forever I told myself.

CH. 2

Stalemates was the nicest cafe and our favorite hangout spot. With varnished oak-wood floors and natural light coming in from the sky view in the center, it was like an outdoor haven but inside. Plus, it's the only cafe where we could go for great coffee and Iced-Frappes. We were basically regulars, if you didn't know any better, you'd think we owned the place.

It took me roughly 10 minutes to get there, and it

didn't take me long to spot Ethan either. There he was flip flops and khaki shorts on exposing his beautiful, well-built legs with a simple teal V- neck tee that hugged his muscles well.

"What a man" I thought to myself. I must have been staring for a while because suddenly Ethan was directly in front of me with a puzzled look upon his face.

"Are you alright man?" He asked.

"Oh sorry, I kind of spazzed out there, didn't I?"

"You sure did bro, wonder what you were thinking about?" He said with a raised eyebrow as he ushered us across the road.

"Nothing really" I said sheepishly.

"Sure, probably got some girl on your mind huh?" Ethan said while flashing a smile that melted my very core.

"Something like that" I mumbled as we made our way inside and grabbed a corner table.

"You look really good by the way, if I had known this was a date, I'd have dressed up more, now people are gonna think you're hanging out with a bum bro."

I shook my head. He could be such an idiot. Heck, I wished this was a date. "You sure are delusional man, keep dreaming. Plus, you always look good."

"Damn, are you saying I'm not your type bro? Way to shut me down." Ethan said as he smirked at me.

I hated when he did that. I could never tell whether we were joking around as usual or if he was serious.

"Hey, you, okay? You seem a little out of it suddenly."

"Huh? Yeah, I'm good, don't worry about it. It's nothing." I said as I checked my phone.

Shortly after, a server, one we'd never seen before came over with two drinks in hand.

"Two iced frappe with hazelnut and vanilla with a hint of cinnamon" she said placing the drinks on the table.

Chuckling, Ethan asked "Are you new here? Don't think I've seen you around before."

"Yes, I am, and they told me all about you two, your scones will be out shortly as well" she said as she turned to leave.

"Well, I'll be damned" I said and then we both started laughing. "Man, they sure do know us huh"

"Facts, ahh man anyway it's so nice to see you, I felt like it's been forever with us."

"That, Ethan I can definitely agree with" I took a sip of my iced frappe then asked, "so what's new, now that you're not working, what do you plan to do now?"

"Straight to the point huh, damn not even a minute to just relax eh Deon?"

"I didn't mean it that way, I just want to know" I said quickly. I totally loved it when called me Deon, the way it rolled off his tongue when he was slightly annoyed at me made me want to hold him close.

"Snap out of it!" I said to myself, "he's talking to you".

"- and I hate to be the bearer of bad news, I mean it's good news I guess because any opportunity is a good opportunity but I'm leaving for University, going to go study and all that now, get my bachelor's degree and-"

"Wait what!" I interjected when I finally caught on to what he was saying. "I thought you didn't want to go. Weren't you saying that you wanted to do your own thing, follow your own vision? What about the schools we had planned to go to?" I said flustered and frustrated.

"Deon, calm down, it's not the end of the world,

it's only a few years away and I'll come back for holidays or Christmases when I can. I really don't have a choice in the matter."

"Wow, just wow. I really can't believe that you're going to fucking leave just like that" I said, fully aware that it wasn't his fault and that I was acting irrationally. Yet for some strange reason I was hurt, I was mad, I felt betrayed but by who? It wasn't his fault so why am I taking it out on him. I know his situation better than anyone else, what his parents are like.

"Fuck, I need to bring the reigns in, now is not the time for me to be lashing out at him" I said to myself.

There was an air of silence as the server brought over our scones, I thanked her and watched her leave.

"I'm sorry man" I said "I was kind of out of turn with that, I know it has nothing to do with you, I just didn't, I don't know, just wow man"

"Yeah, you kind of attacked me man, I feel like there's something else we need to talk about, what's really bothering you?"

Should I? Should I risk our friendship? I know he says he doesn't mind gay people; he says he likes gay friends but I'm not just a friend, we're like best pals, and I'm hopelessly attracted and in love with him.

He's made clear indications that another man is just not appealing to him, but I need to tell him, I need to get this burden off my chest. I've told Davis, my only other straight male friend who I was in love with but with him I was real from the get-go. With Ethan, I've been lying, piecing together the truth and leaving out the rest of the puzzle. "What if he hates me? What if he ends up feeling betrayed?" The last thing I'd want to do is hurt the only other person I've come to love and trust" It was now or never, don't let this summer go and you haven't told him the truth.

"So, are you going to tell me what's the real deal?" "Huh? Oh I... uhm well you see..."

"Deon what is it? Just talk to me normal bro"

"I... I'll just miss you, ok? Like I'll really miss you and I don't know how I'll cope, you guys are all going away and doing things and I'm stuck here. I just, I just... I love you and I'll miss you man" I managed to say. Not what I wanted, I totally fumbled.

"Oh Deon" he said as he got up and gave me a hug, "It's alright brother, we've still got time before I leave, we got so much more to do and I'm always here for you"

"Yeah... we still have time" I said embracing his warmth, his scent and his touch.

I really need to tell him honestly how I feel but for now it's I opted to enjoy this meant with the boy I truly believed I loved, over some frappe and scones.

CH. 3

I'd never felt a warmth embrace as much as the one I felt that evening at Stalemate's Coffee Corner. His arms embracing me as I leaned into his chest, listening to the rhythmic beating of his heart.

This reassurance, this sense of protection and care was like a comforter in the cold of the night. His scent, intoxicating and overwhelming all my senses, like a drug I was high on it, on him.

After the whole Cafe situation, I couldn't get

Ethan out of my head. "Did I sense something? Or was that his general concern for me? I know I tend to read into things more than I should but what if I did feel something? Shouldn't I pursue it?"

Thoughts flooded my head as I stared out the window of my room. It was shaping up to be a hot day as the sun gleamed at me through open windows. I rolled over and checked the time, it was already five minutes to eleven and here I was, still in bed not sure about anything, confused about everything.

"Fuck!" I said wishing that it was easy to ignore my feelings as easy as it was for me to ignore my chores and work obligations. I might as well start my day I thought, slowly pushing myself out of bed. First things first, a long, cold shower to combat my flustered state which I see to be in a lot these days, then a trip to the laundromat and then maybe the grocery store. I think cooking might help take my mind off things today.

It was now half unto the hour of twelve and I was finishing up at the laundromat. I folded my clothes, put them in the basket and took them to my car. I rarely ever drive unless I had quite a bit to do and today was one of those days. There was a grocery store right around the corner, but I wanted to take a drive out of town a bit, to Little Paloozas Market Square. A quaint little place with a friendly atmosphere and some of the best, fresh produce south of the city. Plus, it was only about thirty minutes or so drive from my flat, so it was fine. The drive out of town might just be what I need to clear my mind.

Buildings were replaced by groves and orchids, sidewalks slowly dispersed until all you could see were meadows and livestock. The air clean and fresh, I at once found myself relaxing as the scenery before me calmed my nerves.

"Should probably think about finding a home out here, it's nice" I said to myself. I arrived at Little Paloozas and took a trip to the mini mart to pick up a few spices and herbs. Next stop was the fish market, I think tuna or dolphin today. Turns out they had neither of what I wanted except for whale and pufferfish. I settled on whale, because pufferfish was unchartered territory for me and I didn't feel like stepping out of my comfort zone today in terms of cooking, then I continued along my path. There were so many people here all greeting each other, talking about the latest news around town I presumed. I passed the meat market, not interested in the slightest since it's been about four years since I started my Pescatarian journey.

Finally, the last stop on my checklist was the fresh produce market. I think everyone visits Little Paloozas just for this, everything was so bountiful, I felt like I could take a few of everything. I got some oranges for fresh juice, some tomatoes and greens for a salad and a couple fruits for when I feel snacking. If I wandered around anymore, I might go over my budget so taking that as a sign, I turned around to go back to my car, taking in the scenery as I did.

Shortly after rearing to go, I heard, "DEONDREEEEEEEE" so loud that I almost had a panic attack. "It can't be" I said to myself, "I recognize that voice and obnoxious shouting but that's simply impossible"

I turned around just in time to see the running figure approaching me, I dropped my bags and before I knew it, I was screaming "ALIESHAAAAAAA!"

CH. 4

"Oh, my freaking gosh, how is this possible?" I said hugging her tightly as she jumped on me. I twirled her around for a few, until I set her down and kissed each of her cheeks twice then once on her forehead, it was my way of greeting her. My little jedi, the 'inner bad bitch' as I'd often call her, she was my soul sister, and with her things usually got a bit wild.

"Last I heard you were still in Monte Carlo, getting ready to sail out on another expedition"

"Listen darling, I got back today. I was feeling homesick, and I just couldn't do another long venture. I was here grabbing some lobster and believe it or not I was going to pop up by you because I know you go nowhere on a Saturday."

"Ha-ha sure and I bet you wanted me to prepare you a lobster lunch too huh?" "You're as sharp as ever" she said with a sly smile.

"Did you drive, or do you want a ride?"

"I don't mind the ride, as long as you don't mind bringing me back here after."

"No problem, let's go then." I said picking up my bags and heading back to my car. "You can even crash and spend the night, just like old times"

The drive back was quick, and we were now at my flat on Sankerts Street. It was midday and the heat from the sun scorched the air. Would have been nice to visit the beach today I thought.

"Bloody hell, it's mad hot, isn't it?" Aliesha said.

"Don't worry I've got ice cream, that should cool you down" "My hero" she said smiling as we made our way to my door.

I fumbled for my keys, unlocked the door and led her inside. I took the bags to the kitchen and turned on the AC.

"You've done well for yourself Deondre; this flat is gorgeous! The interior designs are so you. I'm loving the open space and pastel color coordination you got going on here"

"I try" I said while grabbing two wine glasses and a bottle of VOGA Moscato. "I wouldn't be much of an interior designer if I couldn't decorate my own space now, would I?"

I poured out the wine and handed her a glass, "Make yourself comfortable, I'll be with you in thirty."

Then I went back into the kitchen, turned on my oven and took out my whale meat, made light work of seasoning it and setting it aside.

Then I made the salad and tossed it into the fridge. Next was the lobster, boiled, cut in half and seared with garlic butter and lemon juice. That should do it. Then I popped my whale into the oven, fifteen minutes and that was that. I got us plates, served the meals and then joined her in the adjoining living room.

"Thanks darling, I swear in another life you're a chef, this looks amazing."

"A chef? Ha-ha you flatter me, but I'd never cut it." I said taking a bite of my meal.

We laughed and drank and talked about the good old days. After finishing college, she had immediately left for the seas and never looked backed since. Being in one place never suited her and I remembered how as kids she'd always talk about how much she wanted to explore the world. I was super proud of her because she made her dreams come through despite how hard it was in the beginning for her. Aliesha never did too well on her own and for the first couple of months, she'd call in tears, saying how she's tired and that she just wants to pack up her bags and come back home.

Of course, I never allowed that to happen. I was her rock and however I could help, I did. Eventually she stopped being afraid and became so fearless that I looked up to her. There was never one thing tying her to a specific place or at least that's what she told me. She told me all about her adventures and trips around the world. Said she'd never quite gotten over the fact that it's so different out there but so similar in some ways.

I sat and I listened to her as she went on and on. A

much-needed distraction and I was grateful for it. I lived vicariously through her tales of adventure as she described places and moments to me. I made a mental note that sooner rather than later, I would have to start traveling more. I smiled, wondering what could be in store for me out there, excited and terrified all at the same time.

CH. 5

It was well into the afternoon by now and I took our plates into the kitchen and cleared them up, I refilled our glasses, grabbed the ice-cream, two spoons and took a seat.

"Mint chocolate chip, somethings never change with you." Aliesha said gleefully.

"I don't know what people have against this flavor, but it will always be top tier to me." I said taking bite. "I can say the same thing about you too."

"What's that supposed to mean?"

"Well, you do all these great things, see all these amazing places and meet all these interesting people yet you've somehow managed to never had any romantic interests or relationships. Or maybe you do, I haven't seen you in a few years, but you've never once mentioned a boyfriend or any guy for that matter."

"Well, that's not entirely true, I mean I've dated guys. Also, you remember Andrew, I was with him for a while."

"If you mean for a while being three weeks and two days." I said laughingly. "To be honest, I think you've got some commitment issues, or at the very least your personality is just too much for most guys."

"Aren't you the cheeky one! For your information, I don't have commitment issues and I am perfectly capable of being with a guy long term. It's not my fault most men are complete idiots." Aliesha retorted. "Plus, I've totally got..."

I looked at her waiting for her to finish her statement, but she went completely silent and took a sip of her wine. Strange I thought to myself. That's totally unlike her. I wonder what she's hiding or perhaps I said something I shouldn't have.

"Hey, I'm sorry if I said something out of turn. I'm sure you don't have commitment issues; I was just teasing you for old times' sake."

"Oh, it's nothing. You're a total sweetheart. It's just me. I guess I'm not that good of a person." She said with a half-smile. Suddenly she clasped her hands and shook her head. "Anyway, what's new? How is everyone? When last have you spoken to Davis, and are you still head over heels for Ethan, or did you finally come to your senses?"

I could totally tell that something was up and that she was deflecting but her last question totally took me by surprise. I took a long drink of my wine as I avoided her eyes. Aliesha can be a bit direct, caring and honest to a fault, so much so that it hurts. Yet she's been by my side since high school, and she's been there to nurse my wounds after I willingly walked into minefields of emotional damage. I pondered whether I should tell her about Stalemates, I'm not very keen on lying but I really wasn't up for reliving it entirely.

", I talked to Davis a couple of months ago. You know how we are. We're in the part of our friendship where we no longer need the constant communication. He's got his own things to deal with and friends from before me that he's catching up on. He never fails to send me pictures of adventures he's on though. He's a lot like you in that department."

"That's Davi alright, good to see some things truly never change. I've got to pay him a visit in Guam sometime."

"Same but my personal time off will be over soon, so that would have to wait. Plus, I think he said he's planning a trip back home sometime, so I might not have to even bother with going to see him."

"Uh-huh and what about the other question I asked you, you're not getting off that easy."

I sighed, "Well I tried telling him how I felt a few days back but that didn't turn out so well, I think I love him even more now and I think maybe he might care for me or as usual it could all just be in my head and I'm seriously overthinking it as usual. You know me, a glutton for punishment and unrequited loves."

I told her about the Stalemate's Coffee Corner morning, the fact that he's leaving and the hug and everything I felt, sparing no detail as it was impossible for me to forget. After I finished there was this silence, she had a this look on her face that I didn't quite understand. She's been having a lot of these looks lately but I just couldn't read her.

She just stared at me, concern flooding her face, sadness in her eyes but I didn't know why. She came closer and I was confused until she took her hand and wiped the tears from my eyes that I didn't know were there.

"Oh Deon, I'll never understand why you do this to yourself, you're so much smarter than that and you deserve a love and a person of your own where you don't have to question whether the feeling is mutual or not. I love Ethan too… I mean he's a good friend and he's been the center of your growth lately; you've made leaps and strides because he's been there for you, while Davi and I physically couldn't but you can't keep doing this."

She paused suddenly like she had more to say. I knew she wouldn't say what she wanted to, all my life regardless of people being honest with me, they always held back. Everyone felt that I was fragile, and they're right, emotionally I'm weak, it used to be my strongest point, my father surely believed that, and I did too but these days it seems like I'm just weak.

However, I needed to know, I needed her brutal honesty even if I knew I wouldn't like the outcome.

"Say it" I said, frustrated that everyone coddled me like a little child. That they felt the need to nurse my wounds, "Just say it and get it over with."

There was another moment of silence before she said what she had to, I wouldn't like it I said to myself, I should just tell her forget it.

Too late.

"Ethan will never love you the way you want to, he will never be yours in that way. For fuck sakes, he's in love with someone else, a girl that he plans to spend his whole life with, you know it. He's even mentioned it and someday he hopes that he can make things clear. He confides in you; you know he's never going to love you and you are honestly stupid if you think otherwise."

Her words sank like a knife into my heart, those words of hers, twisting and utterly gutting my insides before releasing.

"Listen honey" she was speaking again now, "I was just saying, because you need to know the truth and there's something…"

I couldn't let her finish, I felt horrible as I got up

and I could barely look her in the face, "I'm going to my room, you can stay or whatever you know your way around" I said walking away.

"Deon, I'm sorry but…"

"I'm fine, I just need rest, I'm quite tired. If you want to leave, you can use my phone and call Ethan, he'll give you a lift home."

Nothing else was said that evening. I took to my room and locked the door. Not that Aliesha would come inside, strangely enough this was the only time she respected boundaries. A few minutes later I heard her talking outside. Then a knock on my door and I heard her speak.

"Ethan is coming, I'm headed home, I'm sorry Deon, I worry and care about you and I want you to know that I never meant for any of this to happen. Take care of yourself okay"

Another moment of silence then I heard her walking away, and then I heard my flat door closing. I rolled over to my side, and I let the tears flow, and I let my cries out. I was hurt, broken and I knew that. All the things she said were true, but I didn't care. It was impossible for me to ignore my feelings; I couldn't help that I wanted someone who may never want me, but did that mean I was supposed to give up on ever hoping? On ever dreaming of a future where things are different? I set my alarm, turned on my music and rolled over again.

"Am I not allowed to love?" It was the last thing on my mind, as I faded off into slumber and nothingness.

CH. 6

A few days passed and I had ignored everyone completely and by everyone, I mean Ethan and Aliesha included. Why? Simply because I couldn't face Aliesha, and to be quite honest I didn't want to more so because I'm guessing she told Ethan, because that same evening after she left, he started ringing and messaging my phone.

I saw the missed calls, the texts but I had better things to focus on and honestly, I felt it was best to get myself some space from them for a while and simply clear my head. It was a new week and my personal time off was over, I had quite a few clients for the month and a salon to redecorate the following week, so I figured I'd head into the office and see what I need to handle.

At age twenty-eight, I'd never seen myself having an office. In all actuality, I'd never envision much for myself outside of what I loved to do. I always figured I'd work for someone else; I didn't expect my career to take a turn where I was the boss and ran my own business. I didn't want an office really; I was quite content with working from home but with the more work I took on the more it became harder for me to manage it. So, I got a building, and an assistant, Geneva, that manages it all for me along with two other interior designers, Dianne and Shian.

Geneva was quite a lovely woman, quite meticulous and fashionable. I must admit when she came for the interview two and a half years back, I wanted to hire her on the spot just because of her looks and unique fashion style. Regardless of that, her work ethic and managerial skills were three times what I could manage. Not to mention, that she was very organized, she made my clutters seem like nothing. So, she got the job and has been a great friend and asset to me ever since.

I could bet I had an earful to get from her too because I'm sure somewhere amid me ignoring calls, Geneva was there among them. I pulled up to my building and parked in my reserved spot. We had three floors, a spa on the second floor along with a photo studio, safe to say I value their services a lot. The base floor currently was just a lobby with a few spare rooms to rent. I noticed we had a fresh coat of paint and a couple more signs up. There were also more vehicles than I'm accustomed to seeing.

"The building looks brand new", I mumbled to myself "definitely gonna get an earful now."

I walked in and was greeted by Jean, our receptionist.

"Hey Mr. White, it's been a while. How are you?"

"I'm quite fine Jean, and for the last time just call me Deondre, I admire your formality, but we've been working together for almost 3 years"

"I keep forgetting that. Sorry sir." He blushed.

Poor kid, he had the biggest crush on me. Oh, the irony that I would know just how he feels I said to myself, lost in thought again.

"Oh, how do you like the new additions?" He said glancing towards the left end of the lobby.

Puzzled, I focused my vision and noticed that one of our vacant rooms was bustling with activity.

"Sweet right? We've got a new salon and a lounge area with a cafe that extends behind from the left of the building behind me and stops at the right end of the hall. So, there's like a whole hallway behind me now."

I wasn't even aware of the people waiting in the lobby area and sitting in what appears to be our new lounge and cafe. Now I was seriously questioning how long I was out for or if I even owned this building again. I took a mental note of everything Jean said and decided that I needed to give these two a raise and a vacation.

I took the elevator up to my floor, all the while preparing for the tongue lashing, I was about to get.

CH. 7

I arrived and saw Geneva at her desk, most likely going over some paperwork. "Well, if it isn't the ghost owner of this building himself. Awake from your eternal slumber now?" She said without even looking up at me.

"Ahh well, I figured you wouldn't miss or need me too much" No response.

"I like what you've done to the place" Noticing the nice, elegant changes in the office, "and I see we've had some new additions to the lobby."

"There's a lot you can do in two months and some if you do some work. Plus, this building needed to generate income on your off days as well because you don't work every day of the week and with you being on your much needed vacation, I thought no time like the present."

"Okay I deserve that and I'm sorry, sorry I ignored your calls, I wasn't in a good mind frame. You know me."

"All too well" she said finally looking at me, with a faint smile. "I'm over it, we can go over all the details of what you've missed and how we've grown financially and how well the business is booming later but it's good to see you."

"Oh, Dianne and Shian handled your clients while you were gone, there's none scheduled until the salon next week, so I gave them some time off. Also, you need to get ready for a meeting in twenty, that trainee you were supposed to deal with last week is on his way over. I buzzed him the moment your car pulled in the driveway. He's been here every day since then waiting on you by the way.

"Also, you might want to freshen up a bit, you

look like a hot mess and the world of troubles, boy troubles I presume." she said, barely glancing at me behind the frames of her glasses.

"Ha boys, you know I'm not dating a soul, why would I ever have boy troubles." I said, a blatant half lie but a lie, nonetheless.

"Right." she said rolling her eyes.

Why do I even bother trying to lie to her I'd never know but I enjoyed our little banter. I really left all decision making up to Geneva because she earned the right to, and her loyalty was irreplaceable. If anything were to happen to me, I just know that the business and everyone would be in good hands.

"Thanks, remind me to give you and Jean a raise" I said entering my office. "Already did, the write ups are on your desk, just to approve" she said laughingly.

I chuckled. She really was a life saver. I settled into my chair and stared at the memos on my desk. I spent the next fifteen minutes signing off on reviews and updates then I took the next five to prepare for my meeting with Alejandro Marcello. Apparently, I had approved a scheduled interview a week ago and he's been here every day since. He's tenacious, I'll give him that and I also need to deeply apologize as well, I was already supposed to be back at work, but life had other plans of toying with me first it seemed. I looked over his portfolio and his work were artistic, very traditional and contemporary.

Why he wants to work under me I have no idea, from the looks of it he's already doing extremely well. He wasn't too easy on the eyes either, well that's what I gathered from my social media search. There wasn't much to go on besides his work and it seems he has some heavy connections as well. Strange, I thought, someone of this caliber sure as hell doesn't need to work for me.

CH. 8

"Deondre your appointment is here, sending him in", I heard Geneva as she popped in with freshly brewed coffee and scones from the new cafeteria, we have no doubt. As she left, I heard her say right this way.

She was replaced by a tall, lean physique, chiseled jaw line, and penetrating hazel brown eyes in rolled up jeans, loafers and a dress shirt that slightly exposed his bare chest and an assortment of crystal necklaces. His hair was up in one with a few strands falling to the side and he sported a tattoo on his left arm which I could only assume followed all the way up as a sleeve.

"Ciao Mr. White, nice to finally meet your acquaintance" he said, the thick Italian accent rolling off every word.

My heart stopped; my social search did not prepare me for this. I was taken aback by the stallion of a man that stood in my office. It's not often I find men alarmingly attractive but the man that stood in front of me was nothing shy of perfection in the appearance department.

"Good day, Mr. Marcello. Nice to meet you as well, and first let me apologize for the long wait and my absence from the office."

"VA bene, that's no problem, your reputation precedes you, you're a very busy man and I didn't mind waiting, I think it'll be worth it in the end" he said boastingly as he took a seat.

Oh, a cheeky one, well isn't this refreshing. Just my luck I thought.

"So, I looked over your portfolio and to be quite honest it is beyond extraordinary. There are some very beautiful pieces that you've done, and I see you're into remodeling and design and not just décor. Frankly I think that you're too good to not be working for yourself and why you'd even consider working under me is mind boggling even to me. You're very good at what you do."

"Ah work for you, is that what it says on there?"

Puzzled by his response, "yes that's what is outlined here." I said while handing it over to him.

He laughed and flashed a brilliant smile that I couldn't help but blush, which I immediately regretted and looked away. Last thing I needed right now was a handsomely, devilish guy to drive me insane. There's already one in my life that does exactly that.

"I'm honored, that you think so highly of me and my work, but I'm not interested in being under you as interesting as that may sound." he chuckled. "It seems my meeting here might have been under the guise of something else and I may need to get a new assistant as well."

"So, what are you here for, if not to work for me?" I said with raised brows.

"Your work is revolutionary, the way you incorporate old aesthetic with modern styling is nothing short of amazing. There always seems to be a story to tell as you enter a room that you've designed and that is a remarkable ability and one that I'm not ashamed to say that I don't have."

"You flatter me, Mr. Marcello." I said, not that I wanted him to stop anyway, any form of compliment right now was appreciated. "So, what is it you're getting at?"

"I haven't even begun to flatter you enough but what I propose is, that we join. Your creative story telling design and love for the old arts with my Italian network and resources would be a match made in the stars, signor."

That Italian again, it's like a wave of ecstasy rushing over and in you. I stirred in my chair unable to stop my body from reacting. Why was he making me so uncomfortable I found myself wondering. More pressing matters to attend to I reminded myself and somehow gathered myself.

"You've sure got a way with words, and this all sounds very beautiful and inviting but I'll need some time to think about this and I'd need to hear more than just sweet whispers and flattering words." I said standing up.

"A hard one to pocket I see, but fear not, I plan to win you over yet. You're closed

midday on Saturdays, so how about lunch next Saturday if you're not busy, while we talk some more about what I have to offer and what I can do for you and you for me?"

"I think that's fair, sure no problem" I said shaking his hand. Wow what a grip, it sent instant sensations throughout my body, and I pulled away a little too quickly.

"Do take care Mr. Marcelo, see you on Saturday." I said as I led him out my office. "Oh, please call me Alejandro, I'll text you the location to meet or you can text me your address and I'll come pick you up. My contact info is in your file on me I presume."

"Yes, it is, and you can call me Deondre then."

"Ah and Deondre, I'll make you mine. Call it a gut feeling but you're a partner worth having I just know it." He said smiling as the elevator door closed and he was on his way.

Stunned by his last statement, I stood there both dumbfounded and intrigued by this complete mystery of a man.

"Almost sounds like he's got the hots for you."

Geneva said after a while

"Almost" I said right back, anxious about next Saturday. "So, I'm done for the day, right?"

"When are you ever not done for the day, get out of here, we've got it covered." "Thanks Gen, what would I ever do without you, really"

"Mmhmm, I know."

CH. 9

With an evening off, a trip to Stalemates Coffee Corner for a frappe and a scone seemed like a perfect way to just unwind for the rest of the day.

In the middle of the week, Stalemates always seems to have a crowd, which was fine by me, I liked to rake everything in every now and again, to look at people having a great time. I can't recall when, but I developed a habit of people watching, whether it was at a café or at the park, I quite enjoyed watching others go about their daily routine. I realized that it sounded a bit stalker like, but it was anything but that, inspiration just came in many forms to me. I placed my order for a mocha frappe and some cheese scones and took a seat in the far corner because I'd rather not be disturbed or seen for that matter.

Looking back at everything, this place truly holds a lot of memories for me, back when I was working here part time, that's how I met Ethan. He came around with some people that I knew but he wasn't much of a talker then. He'd just sit there and stare and on the off chance I'd hear him laugh or engage in a conversation with the others.

o o o

His staring went on for weeks, and I guess that's where my interest in him peeked. One day he came by himself and was waiting on the others. I was going on my break at the same time, I had a frappe and some scones, and I sat a little distance away from him. After a while he asked me for a phone call because the others were taking quite a long time to get here.

After the call, he took a seat right next to me, of

course I didn't mind but I didn't know what to make of it as he just stared at me.

I offered him one of my scones, he said sure thing. I warned him that these were a bit spicy cause of the filling I placed in these ones. He didn't seem to mind at first then I remember laughing hard.

"What" he said as he huffed and puffed.

"Your face is red and you're sweating" I said laughingly, "you're not much of a heat fan, are you?"

"Oh," he smiled "it just caught me off guard that's all, but these are really spicy, they're good but real spicy."

I was going to grab him a drink but before I knew it, he was drinking my frappe. I looked at him with amusement on my face, rather brave of him I thought.

He apologized quickly but I said it's alright. Apparently, a mocha frappe was one of his favorite drinks and he got carried away once the flavor touched his lips.

"You can have it" I said.

"Really? Thanks man, I'm Ethan by the way."

"Yeah, I know, you're here almost every other day with John and the others."

"Oh right" he laughed.

Strange guy I thought to myself, yet it was super easy to talk to him. As we talked some more, I realized that he was close to me now, there was hardly any space between us then his leg brushed against mine as he was telling me something and I froze for a while expecting him to say sorry or pull back, but he just kept talking.

It's the closest I'd ever been to someone in a long time, and I was bewildered by the mystery of him. I pulled back and said my break was over. As I was getting up, I saw John and the others, so I told him the gang is here, so he no longer must wait.

They all greeted each other, I talked to John awhile and then they were headed off to the park. So, I got back to work. When I turned around, he was there staring at me again. So, I asked him what's up, if he needed something. He told me thanks for the frappe and that he owes me one.

"No big deal" I said, "I'd say we're even; I mean to be fair, I kind of did almost destroy your mouth with my fire scones"

"Right" he said as he was about to leave, "still I owe you one Deondre, later, I'll shout you."

From then on, it was frappe and scones at Stalemate whenever I was on break or when I was at work. Even after I left there to finally do my own work, we'd still find ourselves here every now and again. We went from Instagram banter, sharing memes and things we liked to chatting on the phone.

Hanging out with John and the others became like a regular thing too. Drives on weekends and…

o o o

I was interrupted by the server as she brought my order. I paid immediately; gave her a tip and thanked her. Stalemate really held irreplaceable moments for me.

I made quick work of my scones and took my frappe to go, I admit that all the nostalgia was getting to me a bit. On my way out I noticed Ethan at a corner seat, and I wasn't the least bit surprised. It was one of his favorite spots too and I bet he thought he'd find me here as well.

"Should I say hi, I mean it's only fair right" I was mumbling to myself. Just as I was making my way over there, I realized that he was holding hands with someone, I tried making a quick turnaround, but it was enough for me to see and to be seen.

She pulled her hand back and he turned around, slightly shocked to see me, "Deondre, hey."

"Oh hey, I'm just on my way out, I've got a busy workload being away from the office so long, so later"

"Deon, hey wait a minute, come on, it's…" his voice trailed off.

"I really got to go, take care Ethan, Aliesha" I barely waited for a response before I bolted out the door.

Ethan and Aliesha, an item. Since when and why they never brought it up. The girl he's been in love with forever is her? When was I going to ever know? Thoughts flooded my mind.

"Argh, I sure as fuck didn't need this" I said out loud as I got in my car and drove off.

The sight of the two of them, a bitter taste like the mocha frappes I loved so much.

CH. 10

That night I can't recall how long I spent in the shower, I'm not even sure how I got out. I kept running what I saw at Stalemate's through my mind, wondering how long it's been going on, if maybe I imagined it.

"No, you definitely did not imagine it", I heard myself say.

I felt betrayed, but why? Why should I feel betrayed, it's not like I was in a relationship with any one of them, I mean they're free to date if they want, I can't control their decisions but still I couldn't help but feel betrayed, like a complete fool.

I made it to the kitchen and decided I needed a drink. I reached for the wine but decided I needed something stronger. I searched my cabinet and managed to find a bottle of vodka I received as a gift from a client.

"I guess this would do."

I took the bottle and headed out towards the porch. It was a starry night but besides that there wasn't much else to see besides the neighboring flats. I poured myself some vodka, straight and took a huge gulp.

"Argh", I coughed then chuckled.

I'm out of my element here, yet the feeling as the liquid burning through my chest towards my stomach was exactly how I felt and in some strange way it made me feel better.

The night air rushed over me and sent chills all over, I felt cold, lonely, bitter maybe.

Then I remembered the Italian, Alejandro, one good memory of the day I suppose and I apparently, have got a date on Saturday, a measly two days away.

"Well, it's not like it's a date, it's just lunch while we discuss his business proposal

"Yeah, but it could be a date, I mean what's to say there isn't something else there?

"That's your problem, you always overthink and see things that aren't there.

"Jeeze, you're hopeless you know that!"

"Yeah", I mumbled to myself. I really am completely hopeless. How did I even find myself in this mess? Oh, I know, I'm an expert at ignoring red flags. I poured myself another glass of vodka. That wasn't all of it, I'm a dreamer, I live in a fantasy world where I think anything is possible.

My father once told me that it's a strength and a weakness, a curse if you look at it. I get what he meant, I built my reputation and career on being a creative dreamer, I was able to achieve interior designs that tell stories because I live in a fantasy. To me that is life itself, a fantasy where I can make anything out of it. Unfortunately, I never learned to separate my work from my reality.

I took another drink before I glanced over at my phone, I hadn't realized it was ringing because I placed it on silent. I checked; it was Ethan. Just ignore him I thought to myself. I ended the call only to realize he'd called several times, along with Aliesha.

I cleared the call logs and noticed a series of texts, mainly saying pick up the phone until I saw one from twenty minutes ago that caught my attention.

'That's it, I'm coming over because we need to talk since you won't respond to my calls and just drove off like that. We're not leaving things like that; you're not just going to avoid me like usual.'

"Shit", not that I could do anything, I gave Ethan a key in case of emergency and for those times he needed some place to crash. "Great, my kindness is coming back full circle to bite me in the ass."

CH. 11

I finished up my drink and decided the best place to continue would be to drink in my room, I doubt I could stomach seeing Ethan right now. A few minutes later I heard a knock on the door.

"Deondre, it's Ethan. I'm coming in okay"

I heard the door unlock, open and then closed. I locked my door, wary of any confrontation or what I might say. My head was now buzzing, and I believe my dear friend, vodka, was finally getting to me.

Should have eaten something, I guess.

"Deondre" I heard him say again, "look I know you're here, your stuffs in the sitting room, the porch door is open, and your phone is there too."

His voice got closer as he neared my door followed by him fiddling with the handle. "Deon. come on, really? This is silly, isn't it?"

Silly, he says. How would he know what silly feels like? I'm the one that's been silly all my life thinking that we could be more than friend. "I don't want to talk Ethan; I've got nothing to say."

"Why though? Because of me and Aliesha? It's not that big of a deal, don't you think you're being a bit unreasonable and childish?"

"So now I'm a child to you", I retorted.

"That is not what I meant, see that is why I didn't tell you anything. Why we didn't tell you anything. I know you'd blow this out of proportion."

"Well, isn't that just peachy, you guys discuss me now? Oh, wait that's incorrect, who knows how long the two of you were dating, so you've both been discussing me way before."

There was silence, which didn't aid in calming me down which was like tossing gas into an open flame and I had just about had it.

"Why'd you do it Ethan? Why'd you guys get together? Why didn't you tell me from the moment you had feelings for her or her for you? You guys are my closest friends, I tell you everything and you guys kept this a secret for how long huh?"

"That's unfair Deon, you don't tell me everything and with me and Aliesha it just happened before we knew it, she came at me, trying to protect you and we got to talking and well here we are."

To protect me. I didn't understand what he was saying, and it wasn't helping that my head was pounding like crazy now. I was beyond outraged or maybe I was just confused. I opened the door and there he was, just standing there, looking at me with concern or maybe it was pity, it felt like pity.

"What do you mean by that, I've never lied to you", an obvious lie, I mean he didn't know how I felt but I was doing that to protect myself. "And protect me? Why would Aliesha have to come to you for that?" He stared at me, and it felt like hours had passed before he opened his mouth again but what he said took me by surprise.

"You never told me you have feelings for me." he

paused, "That you loved me.

"I never wanted to say anything because that was all on you, but I waited to hear it but after a while I just figured it was just fleeting moment. After all I've had some of those moments myself in the past and it really wasn't a big deal, at least to me.

CH. 12

I didn't know what to say, my head was spinning, and I felt like I was losing control. "Ali came to me, to tell me that I should stop leading you on, stop being so close and friendly with you because it would only hurt you in the long run. I asked her what she was going on about, and that's when she got upset and accused me of acting like I didn't know that you liked me, that you were falling for me."

Ali? So, he's got a nickname for her, and he

knows, all this time he knew, and I was just what, some idiot to pass the time? This explains the look Aliesha gave me when we hanged out awhile back, she knew that he knew, she was seeing him and she didn't have the guts to tell me, she just let me feel like crap this entire time.

"To be honest, I kind of figured you liked me, and I expected that you'd fall for me, I just never knew it was that much until she told me. I always thought you'd find someone else, and it wouldn't be that big of a deal. Years went by and you never told me, so I always just assumed you had finally moved on until that night I took Aliesha home from you and she told me what happened. I felt so horrible man, suddenly your behavior at the café made sense and then I realized how hard it must have been for you and that you were trying to tell me on that day." "Deon, look I wanted to tell you, about Ali and everything, it was one of the reasons I came back as well, to clear the air between us because I didn't like hiding this from you man. Bro, I like you, like I really do, and I honestly do care for you a lot; I love you but..."

"How long?" "What?"

"I said how long? How long did you know? How

long did you watch me make a fool of myself? How long were you laughing at me? The hopeless fool that was in love with you? How long? Tell me!", I shouted.

My voice shaking, cracking, holding back the tears that were forming. "Tell me!" I said while I shoved him from my door.

He looked shocked but didn't say anything, he lowered his eyes to the floor, knowing that it wouldn't do me any good to tell me, to answer that question. I didn't care, I needed to know.

"Deon, you're drunk, maybe we should stop for the night, let me get you to bed."

"Don't touch me! For once in your goddamn life just be honest. No more lies. Tell me!" I shouted, pulling away from his hands and stumbling backwards.

"I suspected the first time we met that you weren't like most guys. Then it was a few months into our friendship that I picked up on your feelings for me, the way you'd go out the way for me, the way you looked at me sometimes, like you were lost." he said, his eyes on the floor once more.

"I'm such an idiot." I said laughingly, tears welling in my eyes. Unable to hold them back anymore, I felt them rolling down my cheeks in streams.

He looked up at me, his eyes locked on mine. His expression one of sadness, hurt and worry but all I could see through teary eyes and my clouded mind was pity.

"Deon, I'm so sorry", he reached out to hold me.

"No!", I shoved him back. "I don't believe you."

The tears I could no longer hold back, the pounding in my head louder and faster, I slowly collapsed just in time for him to hold me as I hit the floor.

Everything was fading black, his face, the last thing I remembered as it all went dark.

CH. 13

I opened my eyes and felt a shot of pain fly straight to my brain. "Ugh, a hangover just great."

Note to self, drinking anything other than wine is a sin that should never be committed ever again. When did I change out of my clothes I wonder? I tried moving but that's when I realized that I was being spooned, basically pinned down in a manner of speaking. As I shifted my body, I saw Ethan, on his side laying peacefully right next to me, his other hand cradling me close to him as if I were a child.

I felt warm, safe for the first time in a long time like this was everything I'd needed. Yet I know this wasn't real as much as I wanted it to be.

I smiled, he really was one of the nicest and sweetest guys I'd ever known or met. I dreamed of a day like this, although we've slept in the same bed before, it had never felt so close, so intimate, so safe. His half nakedness triggered an exciting response within me, as I watched his upper body. To be honest this feeling was euphoric that I almost clean forgot about the hangover and the events leading up to it.

"Ethan" I said as soft as possible.

I didn't want to wake him; I didn't want this moment to end. If I could freeze this point in time on a loop, I'd gladly trade all my possessions and gifts just for that. Look at me being silly again; why I would give up everything for him I still couldn't understand. If this is what love is like, then this is fucking stupid. Here I was acting like what I tell countless of my peers. not to be 'hung up' on someone when the feeling isn't mutual or being reciprocated.

Gosh, what is wrong with me? Get a grip, I told

myself mentally, there's no future in this, there won't be an us.

"Hey" I said again, this time tapping him. No response. Maybe I could let this moment be a little longer I thought to myself. I shifted myself so I was back to how I was and nested a migraine that I could feel still lingering.

I don't know when I drifted off back to sleep or how much time had passed but I felt the warmth of his breath on my neck, and I realized we were closer together than before. I felt his entire weight against me, not that I minded but I just couldn't bare it no more. I turned to wiggle myself out from under him but as if by instinct he pulled me close and there I was, face to face, the very breath escaping his nostrils rushing over my own face.

I held my breath, my heart beating faster than normal as I realized just how close we were. His lips, just 2 inches away from mine. I slowly placed my hand on his body with all intent of pushing myself off, but his skin felt smooth as I trailed my fingertips across his chest. He'd always tease me but never, not even once had I ever troubled or teased him back, primarily out of fear of rejection or awkwardness but what have I got to lose, I thought to myself now.

It felt sensational or should I say magical just to trail my hands on him as little jolts of electricity rippled throughout me. I looked up again, his lips just right there; I'd dreamed of a moment like this, and I felt like maybe just maybe I could steal a kiss.

In the dead silence I could hear my own heartbeat beating abnormally fast, like a drum solo at an electrifying concert. I pressed my lips slowly against his and for a short moment I felt alive as his wet, soft lips engulfed mine, but I immediately pulled off out of fear.

"This is stupid" I mumbled. "I'm stupid"

I opened my eyes and there were his eyes staring back at mine.

CH. 14

In that instant, I felt so ashamed, so vulnerable. There he was just staring back at me with a quizzical look on his face, as usual I could never truly understand his expressions. The silence between us felt like it went on and on forever, all the while getting more awkward by the minute.

He leaned forward and to my surprise, kissed me softly on the lips, then he pulled off and shook his head.

"You're not stupid" he said finally. "Deon you're the most brilliant person I know, stupid is never something I'd use to describe you."

"I'm sorry I can't be the guy you want me to be, that I can't love and treat you the way you're supposed to be treated and that must suck. I don't know how you feel, and I can't begin to imagine how you feel but I've never once pitied you or felt sorry for you. If anything, I've always been in awe of how strong and free spirited you are.

"You do whatever you set your mind to without holding back, you take charge of your own life without caring what anyone else says and that is something man. Not a lot of people are able to truly be themselves in a world where we're all trying to belong or fit in, but you do that so effortlessly and I love you for that."

"I need some space."

"Oh sorry, my bad I'll let you go now." he said as he released me from his arms. He chuckled. "I sometimes get carried away I know that you're just special to me and seeing you hurt or hurting you is the last thing I'd ever want to do."

"Thanks, but I need some space, some time to

myself if you don't mind. I don't think I can handle this right now, but I appreciate what you've said and all that you've done but the truth is you did hurt me, and you lied to me. I admit I didn't confess my feelings to you but those are my feelings, so I never really lied to you. She had no right discussing me with you and what you guys did all this time was just wrong and horrible and I don't know how to feel about that. I'd never expect this from the both of you and I don't know if I could be friends or let alone be around people that can behave in such a way."

I got up and went ahead to the bathroom, my head pounding more and more now. Great, it's back, what a bloody nightmare this is.

"I see..." I heard him say. "Oh, and Ethan?"

"Yeah, Deon."

"Can you leave the spare key as well on your way out, I'd appreciate that."

"Right, okay." his voice lowered now. "Take care Deon and I'm sorry again, I really am even though it seems like I'm not, but I never wanted things to get like this between us. I'm sorry for what I did, and I apologize for the fact that I cannot love you in that role, but I do love you and I always will."

I closed my bathroom door and got in the shower. I turned on the shower head and let the water flow all over me. I didn't even bother with turning on the water heater, the cold blast as it pummeled me seemed to be exactly what I needed.

I sank to the floor. That was the hardest thing I ever had to do, I had already forgiven him and that's what scared me. How could I have forgiven him already in that instant, after all that happened, after being so damn hurt. Tears came flowing again and I cursed myself for being so emotional, for being so soft.

What's done is done is what I told myself. I'd have to handle the choice I made and right now I felt like I made the right one. Plus, I needed my head clear for this meeting with Alejandro that was now just a day away.

My life was one rollercoaster after the other and there seemed to be no getting off it anytime soon.

CH. 15

I heard my alarm go off, reluctantly I rolled out of bed and turned it off. It was Saturday, the day of the meet. I had roughly three hours to get myself ready.

I checked my phone, text messages from Geneva telling me to not forget about today, she wants all the details and remember to have a good time. What a mess I thought but I loved her for it.

A few more messages from Ethan and Aliesha that I ignored. More updates from Geneva about some new prospective clients. Guess I could look at those later. I hooked my phone up to my media player and hit shuffle. As if the universe is having a laugh, 'Gonna Love Me' by Teyana Taylor starts playing. What a riot I told myself.

Now I have no idea where we're going for lunch so deciding what to wear seemed like my top priority. When in doubt, khaki shorts and a long sleeve white, button up shirt with loafers seemed like the most casual/business friendly choice.

I took a shower and had a light breakfast; toast and coffee to get me started. Next, I decided I'd let my hair down, I normally had them up in one, but I decided maybe they needed some freedom as well. A quick wash, leave in conditioner and curl activator was all I needed, and I was set.

My music stopped and I heard, "Incoming call from Mr. Marcelo."

I answered on my wireless headphones, "Hello Alejandro, I'm just getting ready. I'll be ready in 20 minutes."

"Ah, great. Just calling to make sure that we're still on si?" "No problem, where should I meet you?"

"If it's okay with you, I'll come pick you up."

"Sure." I said with ease. Not having to drive would be a much-deserved break to be quite honest. "I'll send my location."

"Great, arrivederci Deondre!"

His heavy yet subtle Italian mixed with English was just as powerful over the phone as it was in person. I quickly got dressed and freshened up and by the time I was done and out my door, he pulled up in a vintage sports car by the looks of it. An Italian thoroughbred through and through I see.

He flashed me a smile as I got into his car. "Nice car you've got here."

"Ah si, Bellissima isn't it?" he said, with such passion that I could only assume this was one of his prized possessions. "A 2020 Alfa Romeo 4C Spider, handles like a baby but let me not bore you with the details."

"You underestimate me, Alejandro."

He looked at me with one elevated brow as if intrigued by my sudden statement. "Oh?"

"She is indeed a beauty, what she lacks with her subpar interior materials and crampy space, she makes up for in her razor-sharp handling, gut-punch acceleration and the fact that it looks striking exteriorly in any color. A head turner for sure.

He stared at me dumbfoundedly, so I continued, "A truly focused sports car with the heart of an Italian in mind. It gives you that vintage sports car feels, some would even say it's romantic in a vintage roadster sort of way, a throwback to simpler times before all the technological advances.

"Powered by a 237-hp turbo four, however it only allows for a six-speed automatic. I see you have the Alpine sound system with subwoofer added a nice touch. All in all, it's a nice car in terms of uniqueness and flair."

The look on his face was priceless to say the least. It was as if he'd taken a blow to his chest, and he was rearing from the side effects. I think I proved my point.

I laughed, "What?"

"You're a man of many talents, I see, and you may have just stolen my heart." "Exaggeration, I simply have an eye for detail, nothing more, nothing less." "Si, and the knowledge of a thousand Magi."

"Magi?"

"Ah yes how do you say it here… wise men or kings."

"You flatter me yet again with such words, but like I said, it's just my love for my craft."

"All the more reason why I want you." he gazed at me for a long moment, an odd gleam in his piercing hazel eyes, before he put his vintage beast in drive. "A partnership of course."

"Uh huh, I see. So where to for lunch?"

He smiled, "Home, mio Amico. Home."

What an interesting guy I thought to myself, an open book yet a complete mystery. I was intrigued by the man himself to say the least. I could only imagine what sort of proposal he had in mind on this partnership as we sped off on the open road, the roar of his car drowning out every other sound.

CH. 16

After what seemed like a seemingly short drive in a fast car on the smooth, open road, we arrived at home as he clearly put it. We pulled into the driveway of a beautiful two story, Italian styled family home with three garages: two on the left-hand side and one on the right with the walkway leading to the door in the middle. Cultural, seems he values his heritage and history very much and what I can only assume was a love of fast cars hidden behind each of the two garage doors on the left.

The air always felt cleaner out in the countryside as I took a deep breath. I stepped out of the car, taking the time to look at the surroundings, noting that certain houses within the area had a familiarity in terms of décor to it. Along the walkway, on each side there grew wildflowers yet they seem to be a rather controlled form of mess with pink rock roses, blue pimpernel and poppy. The colors gave it a certain vibe, as the mash up between the shades of pink, purple, blue and red danced in the midday sun; it was magical to say the least.

"You have a beautiful home. I'm guessing the décor and details are all you?"

He beamed, nodding approvingly as he looked around in awe like he was seeing it for the first time again. Another of his prized possession or accomplishment I presume.

Alejandro opened the front door and led me inside, "Welcome to mia casa, Deondre. Feel free to look around as I park the car in the garage."

"Don't mind if I do."

To the left I noticed the living area, despite having a traditional look, it had a bit of modern simplicity to it as well. I noticed the brick style columns as I stepped down into the living area onto grey hardwood floors. The L-shaped couch in a darker shade of grey with various shades of cushions and pillows occupying the seating. The real gem of this room though that caught my eye, was the center piece table, that included several rectangular, varnished pieces of wood that were fastened and held together by two pieces of black stainless steel on each end.

This house is simply majestic I thought to myself. I had barely moved a muscle when I heard the door close, and Alejandro appeared.

"I take it you've made yourself at home?" he said as he took set down his keys.

"I barely made it passed your living area, your home is definitely amazing, I can just imagine what the rest of the house is like."

"Now you flatter me signor. So, about lunch, I'll treat you to a classic Italian home cooked meal if that's alright with you?"

"No time like the present to try a new cuisine, so have it, I don't mind." "Great, would you like some wine while you wait?".

"I'll take a glass of white wine if you have any." He

disappeared into the right side of the house. "Are you coming? I won't bite." he laughed.

Cheeky little fella isn't he. I followed suit and entered another magical room but with a more traditional scene. If I had a kitchen like this, I might never leave this room I thought to myself.

Various herbs and spices decorated this area. Rosemary flowers in pots graced the windows and windowsills with colors of purple, white, pink and blue flowers. As well as bougainvillea blossoms just outside the window. A totally different color scheme than the living area, a lot of white with brown decal on handles and bowls. Another showstopper for this room that caught my breath were the copper pots and pans hanging above the kitchen island.

I took a seat as he poured me a glass of Prosecco and dawned his apron.

"I've done most of the prep in anticipation of lunch with you today, so it won't be more than another twenty minutes."

I took a sip of my wine, "What are we having?"

"Well to start, we're having Panzanella, and a Mushroom Risotto followed by Pasta Carbonara and for dessert, a Tiramisu and Pistachio Panna Cotta.

The desserts were made ahead of time and the Panzanella so it's just the Risotto and Carbonara that needs finishing."

He said all this while gracefully moving about the kitchen, "I'd ask if you need help but if I didn't know any better, I'd say you were a bonified chef Alejandro."

"Ha, my nana is a chef back home, she owns a little ristorante and me along with my siblings all helped growing up. Cooking was essentially part of who I am. It was a time for family to bond and a way for our nana to instill familial values in us. It was a fun time, there's nothing more important than family and strong bonds. You just relax and let me take care of this."

A family-oriented person huh, I now understand where his strong sense of tradition and roots stem from. I'm certainly not opposed to having a stallion of a man cook lunch for me while I watch either, a win for me.

CH. 17

As I watched him, time seemed to fly by, and he was now pouring me my second glass of wine and serving me Panzanella.

"So, tell me more about this business proposal of yours."

"Not so fast signor, first we eat. This is Panzanella, a salad normally eaten by peasants consisting of two things that are irreplaceable; ripe tomatoes and Italian bread, it's what my Nan often made for us growing up."

Peasant wasn't something I'd use to describe this dish. It was visually beautiful and tasted of fresh herbs with a hint of olive and sesame oil.

"It's amazing" I said as I took another bite. "I'd love the recipe for this if you don't mind sharing?"

"Ah you love to cook as well?"

"I dabble in it, it's fun and it's creative, what's not to love about it?"

The rest of lunch was magnificent to say the least, every dish better than the next and all tasted of home as he so clearly said. We talked about many things, his family, moving out and venturing on his own. The struggles he faced trying to define himself outside of his family name that was known more for their food rather than interior designing. He wasn't dismissive of his family name because with it came connections that helped him to progress as far as he has.

"This is why I propose a partnership with you, I've got the connections and the well-known name but you, you've got the natural talent, the eye for attention to detail, for telling una storia with each placement and design. To be frank I need you and I'm willing to put in all the work to show you exactly how we'd work well together."

I stared at the man before me, pleading and asking for my help, which he didn't need to. I usually trust my gut feeling when it comes to my art and I've done my background work on him, he's very much legit and with large connections across the globe.

"First let me tell you this" I said after a while. "Your work is amazing; it truly captures who you are as a person and where you come from. Albeit, it's also why you're having trouble."

"Eh? cosa intendi? What do you mean?"

"You're stuck in traditional is what I meant, so you can't appeal to the larger market that you have at your disposal. From the beginning of this meet I've sensed everything about you in terms of who you are.

"Your work pays homage to your home and upbringing which is fine, but everyone is different, and in this business, they're looking for something that reminds them of something special to them or something new. Alejandro, your scope to bluntly put it is too small, you need to dream more. You need to put yourself in their shoe, learn their history and background and what makes them unique thus your designs become unique and one of a kind by adding your own personal spin or touch on it."

He sat back in his seat, as if taking it all in was a bit much for him. "I hope I didn't offend you in anyway."

"Ah no, it's not that. Per favore, continue."

"Alright then, I have no problem accepting your proposal because I want to help you and it's mutually beneficial to me as well, a larger clientele would also put me on the map which I don't mind. So why don't we shake on it and then we can go through the proper paperwork on Monday and the extra details that we need to iron out of course?"

I extended my hand to him, and he took it with such strength that I almost lost my balance.

"Ah Deondre, grazie." he said as he pulled me close and kissed my left then right cheek respectively. An Italian custom I'm sure but it caught me off guard.

"You're welcome."

"Time for dessert, shall we take this to the couch and get more acquainted as you tell me about you? I want to know exactly who Deondre is and what he's all about. Although I may

already have my reservations about you."

"Oh, how interesting then, I hope I don't disappoint."

CH. 18

I spent the evening telling Alejandro a bit more about myself, not that it compared to his upbringing. I broke off from my family at a young age, they had high hopes for me, but I always found myself being free spirited and what I wanted was to experience life on my own without being burdened by what was expected of me.

I was on my own for some time and I did various odd jobs here and there but never sticking to one for a long period of time except for my last job where I worked at a café. After a while I got fed up with working for others and decided it was time to be start my own business.

"Did you always know you were going to be an interior decorator?" Alejandro asked, pouring himself another glass of wine.

"Well, honestly no, I wasn't even aware that it was something I wanted to do, let alone that I would be good at. I'd always find myself decorating things and helping my friends out with their new spaces and businesses. Most of what I knew came from watching videos on the net and that HGTV home decorating channel.

"Eventually a friend of mine told me I should start doing videos and documenting it, so I did just that and started posting my work online and it sort of just took off from there and before I knew it, I had enough to invest in myself and fund my business."

"Ah si, I watched your videos a couple of years back. That's how I first came across the raw talent that is Deondre White. I'd never seen such whimsical and fun artistry before, you captivated me in ways I've yet to describe."

"Oh." I said, blushing, unable to hide my excitement at his outright flattery. "You're skillful with your words, aren't you?"

"Ha-ha no at all, I'm just very honest. I may not have an eye for attention to detail like yourself, but I do have an eye and sense for exceptionally fine things." he said as he took our glasses and now empty bottle of Prosecco and headed for the kitchen.

Hot and bothered. Must be the wine I thought, what was that my 6th or 7th glass? Either way it was nice, I can't recall when last I've had such a pleasant and fun time. A short while after, he returned with two small glass bowls filled with a green and white substance, topped with a mint leaf.

"The last of the dessert, the Pistachio Panna Cotta." he said as he handed me a bowl. "Gustare, enjoy."

I took a bite and immediately I fell in love with its smooth texture, the mint a refreshing touch after all that wine. Another bite and the crunch of the nuts and pistachio crumble gave it a nice contrast to the earlier velvety texture.

"You like?" he asked.

"Oh, I love it, this is your best one yet." I mused. "Truly magnificent Alejandro."

He flashed me a smile and took a bite himself. What a peculiar man I thought to myself again.

"So, Deondre, tell me who has your heart? You're an open book but there seems to be nothing about your romantic interests online or anywhere for that matter. You have someone special, no?"

Someone special huh, I thought I did but turns out I was making a fool out of myself for all these years, chasing one person. That would explain the mystery surrounding my love interests, seeing as I've never truly had an actual relationship.

"Did I happen to say something wrong; you seem troubled Deondre. I hope I wasn't too forward." "Oh, no it's not that. Let's just say I thought I loved someone, that I gave them my heart, but it turns out it could never be reciprocated in the way that I wanted it to. So, for years I've been chasing after someone who wasn't even interested in me like that. So no, no one special. I guess I am a tad bit reserved as well, as I rarely have time for anything outside of my own interests."

"Ah, I see." he said. "If I'm wrong please, perdonami for this."

Before I could ask what for, his hand grabbed the back of my neck and his lips encased mine in a swift, soft kiss that sent ripples throughout my body.

CH. 19

In total shock, my body felt numb unable to react to the sudden action of his mouth on mine. His tongue skillfully invaded my mouth and tasted of pistachio and mint as I tasted him. After what felt like an eternity to me, he finally let up, easing back into the couch and taking another bite of his Panna Cotta.

Panting, almost out of breath, I watched him as he so casually went back to eating his dessert. What the heck was that just now? Not that I was protesting it,

I've had a lot of kisses in my lifetime, but none has ever left me panting before, none had tasted so magical. Yet there he was just eating his dessert like he just hadn't try to take my breath away.

Finally, he spoke up, "I hope I wasn't too forward again, but I've been meaning to do that from the moment you sat down in my ride and lectured me so beautifully about my beast of a ride.

"Of course, I didn't know how you'd react or if you'd even take kindly to it but by the looks of it, it seems my reservations about you were right."

There was that overconfident attitude of his again, a very peculiar man indeed. On any other given day, I'd for sure have had an issue with what he did but I was quite enjoying my time with him, and I suppose deep down I've wanted him to make a move. I know I thought about making one several times for the day already.

"And what if your reservations were wrong?" I retorted, trying to collect myself. "Weren't you worried that I'd be offended, and you'd lose a partnership?"

"Well signor, simply means I was wrong, nothing more, nothing less. Plus, you don't seem like the type of guy who'd go back on his word especially when business wise it is beneficial for you, your company and your employees." he smiled cunningly. "A calculated risk, I had nothing to lose except for a chance to see where this would take us and what all we could be, but you had everything to gain."

"It seems I have been figured out and beaten all in one fell swoop." I said reluctantly.

He flashed me a smile that I knew all too well, it's one where you've cornered your opponent and initiated checkmate. The rest of the evening went by just as great. We talked a great deal about his ulterior motives in meeting me outside of work. He basically admitted to pursuing me and we spent the time getting to know one another more. He told me more about his family, his journey in getting here and being away from his family for so long and in return I told him more about me. I eventually told him about Ethan, for some strange reason it was easy to talk to him.

"His loss signor White, you are indeed a rare gem, one hardly discoverable in most people's lifetime."

"Again, with the words, you've got a skillful tongue."

"That indeed I do." he said as he kissed me once more, slowly and this time with more passion than his first one.

CH. 20

The ride back was pleasant. He opted for a slow drive, showing me around his neighborhood and taking me along the more scenic roads. We stopped at Greeks Hill, to enjoy the sunset. The hues of red and orange cascading alongside the blue, adding heavily to the magic of the countryside and to the mystery of Alejandro, an Italian through and through that held my hand, who somehow wanted me in ways I could never imagine or thought possible.

We pulled up to my street and made a right until we got to my flat. He pulled up on the curb and parked his car.

"As much as I'd like to follow you inside, it seems you've got company." he said pointing at the figure waiting by my door. "Plus, I think you may have had enough of me to last you a couple of days."

"My place might pale in comparison to yours either way." I said jokingly.

"Oh, I doubt it, arrivederci amore mio, goodbye for now." he said as he kissed me for the final time that day.

"Oh, and hey who knows, maybe I might have you tomorrow." I said as I got out of his car. "For lunch that is."

The look on his face priceless before he smiled, and he drove away. I walked up to my flat at the figure waiting for me. Aliesha huh, should have figured she'd come around sooner or later.

"I saw your vehicle, so I thought you were home as usual, but I called and no answer, so I figured you went on one of your jogs." she said approaching me. "I tried ringing your cell, but it went straight to voicemail. By the way, who was that you never told me you were locking lips with a such a hottie?"

"Well, I have a life, one that doesn't always involve you or being at your beck and call you know." I said staring at her. "And why do you want to know? Plan on having a secret relationship with that one behind my back too. After all, that's your specialty, isn't it?"

She stopped with her approach, utter shock on her face. I wasn't about to pull any punches just because she's supposed to be my best friend.

"Okay I may have deserved that." "You think?"

"So, no hugs and kisses, Deondre?"

"What do you want Aliesha? I've had a great day and I'd like to end my evening on a good note. So, if you've got something to say then say it so I can get into my flat and get some sleep."

There was silence for a couple minutes and honestly, I was getting rather fed up and a little tired of standing outside. I took out my keys to open my door and that's when she finally spoke.

"I don't know what you want me to say. I'm sorry? Because I am, you should know that I'm sorry, that I never meant for any of this to happen. In all honesty I tried telling you that night, but you wouldn't listen, you complete shut me out like you're doing now.

Hurting you was never my intention, I was always looking out for you, for your best interest."

"You don't get it do you?" I said finally. "It did happen, you did hurt me and saying that you tried telling me that night doesn't justify the fact that you've had multiple chances to tell me for years! I would cry and tell you everything, you knew how I felt about him, and you let me be the fool for years, holding on to something that was never there.

"You were supposed to be my best friend, I knew you before I knew him, we've been together since high school and then you come and play a number on me and try to be a victim? Really Aliesha? Forget the fact that I was silly, hiding my feelings and wishing for something that could never happen. Let's forget the fact that I never told him anything, but you did, and it wasn't your truth to tell. Fuck! How could you be so clueless? Do you know what it felt like watching him tell me he knew all along for years and that's because you told him?"

I was fuming now, and I had all right to be. I'd never blown up on them like this before, I'd never blow up on her before and I realized in that moment that I was hurting more than I cared to admit. The two of them had me like an idiot for years, years of my life wasted chasing something unattainable. All I heard were excuses, talking about they never meant to hurt me. What human being could possibly do what they did and still expect to play victim?

"Deondre, I'm sorry but it just happened, and I didn't know how to tell you and it hurt me to keep this from you and it hurt Ethan even more because I told him not to tell you anything, I wanted you to hear it from me but I, I just..."

"Don't you dare defend him! You didn't know how to tell me? How stupid do you think I am? How hard was it to pick up the phone and call me, or send a text? What kind of person are you really? I don't even know who you are anymore." I said quite frankly. "The Aliesha I know, told me whatever she wanted even when I didn't' want to hear it but you didn't know how to tell me? Bullshit!"

I opened my door and stepped inside. I turned and looked at her, tears in her eyes as she cried that she was sorry repeatedly.

"I need my space, Aliesha; I don't know what to think of you right now and I can't ever forgive you." I said as I closed my door. Another lie, because I'd already forgiven her just as much as I'd forgiven Ethan because when all is said and done, the bonds we share are strong,

they might break but they're mendable. Right now, however, I just couldn't stomach either of them, I couldn't stomach the fact that the boy I had loved, that deep down I still cared about was sleeping with my best friend.

CH. 21

Couple weeks had passed since then, it was now the last Friday in the month June as I found myself in my office, signing off on pay checks and documents. I had Alejandro over on Sunday despite my run in with Aliesha that Saturday night. Another amazing time spent together although he spent most of it aweing about my interior designs. It was as if I was entertaining a crazed fan at the same time.

I cooked of course, nothing fancy and despite

trying to keep him out of the kitchen, he found himself beside me, helping me along the way, teaching me and playfully teasing me on my poor applications of cooking techniques. We watched a movie where I found out that despite his very strong demeanor, he was a child when it came to horror films. I spent the entire evening laughing and bursting out into tears as he jumped at every slight moment or hid his face behind the cushions.

I also got a lecture from him, asking me to make up with my friends because to him it seemed as if I was missing a part of myself every moment, I didn't talk to them. He couldn't understand that I had forgiven them but refused to talk to them or let them know. We debated this for a while but eventually I gave in as he showered me with hugs and kisses, pleading for me to do something about the situation.

We met again a week after that on Tuesday at my Stalemates to go over the details of the partnership and contracts. Stalemates Coffee Corner had become a usual place for us as well, he fell in love with the coffee and scones but the frappes he was having a hard time wrapping his taste buds around. He said I had peculiar taste to say the least.

I had already given Geneva the run down and as usual she had everything ready in time, for when he arrived back at the office with me. It was business as usual; we became partners and he left, saying he'd text me the following evening. Geneva kept smiling at me, wanting to know more of what happened on Saturday but I don't kiss and tell which earned me a scornful eye from her.

Most of my weeks since then were spent with Alejandro occupying about two thirds of my days during the week. When I carried him on projects to give him new perspectives and on my off days which seemed to be complete spent with him at his house. Wednesday, I got down dirty as he gave me a crash course in gardening. Seeing him half naked, tending to plants in the garden was a sight to behold. If there ever was a God, I imagined that's what he would look like as he tended his fields.

I was interrupted by a call from reception, as Geneva was out on lunch and not due back for another twenty minutes or so.

I heard Jean on the other line. "There's that Italian here for you again Mr. White but he doesn't have an appointment." he said sternly.

"That's alright Jean, let him up it's fine. He doesn't need an appointment, he's also the one we're partnering with as I've discussed before."

"Right if you say so. You're free to go up." I heard him say before hanging up the line.

A few minutes later, Alejandro came into my office, kissed me on the cheeks and pulled a chair right next to me.

"I don't think your receptionist likes me very much."

"I think that's because he has a crush on me but and you are kind of a hot topic amongst the tenants of this building."

"Oh really, I wonder where they got that idea from, I've been nothing but discreet at your office." he said playfully.

"Might have something to do with you kissing me in the parking lot of my building, where might I point out, customers walk in and out from."

"Scusa, but the parking lot is fair ground at least it's not in the office."

I rolled my eyes at him; he really was something else as I filed away documents and cleaned up my desk. His Italian with English, enticing me every single time. I could get used to this I told myself, heck I even started learning a bit of Italian since then and Alejandro hardly had to repeat himself in English for me.

"So, are you all ready for this evening?"

"I don't really have a choice in the matter, do I?"

"None at all, il mio amore." he said grinning at me.

Already to go, we got up and made our way to the elevator. I made sure to leave a note to Geneva that I'd be out, but I'd already handled pay checks, and everything was sorted and ready to be distributed.

As we were leaving, I told Jean, to hold all my calls for the rest of the day and send any important messages to my email or give them to me on Monday because I won't be in work this weekend. As if to toy with him, Alejandro held my hand and rushed me out the door. I admit I found his childish side remarkably refreshing and I welcomed it.

CH. 22

We pulled in at Stalemate's Coffee Corner. A place of so many memories, old and new ones, seemed fitting I guess when you think about it. I'm not sure I was ready for this but a part of me knew that it was necessary, and I made a promise to Alejandro, and it was one I intended to keep.

We walked in, found a corner table and took a seat. It was relatively empty as the lunch rush had just finish. Perfect I thought to myself not that it made much of a difference, but I didn't mind the quiet atmosphere for the moment.

"It'll be fine, no need for you to worry, il mio amore." he said as if sensing my agitation.

He held my hands and kissed them gently before locking his eyes with mine until we were interrupted by familiar voices.

"Hey guys."

I looked up and saw Ethan with a soft expression on his face, he looked different somehow and beside him stood Aliesha who obviously looked more nervous than me. Alejandro got up and greeted both, extending a handshake and kiss on each cheek to Aliesha first then to Ethan.

"You must be Alejandro." Ethan said. "The one who contacted me I presume?" "Si, per favore have a seat."

"Hey Deondre." he said after finally sitting down. "How are you doing? You look well." "Hey Ethan, Aliesha. I'm doing great yeah."

The awkwardness was stifling to say the least as the two of them avoided eye contact with each other and with me. Probably to show respect to my feelings I suppose, not that it mattered. Now that they were here, I didn't particularly feel anyhow. I was happy to see them though, even if my attitude was saying otherwise. The silence went on for a while until a waiter came across.

"Oh, it's you guys." she said gleefully. "If I had known, I'd have just brought the usual but seeing as it's company, I guess the orders are different?"

"Uh not really, just get us four of the usual, but make one frappe a mint chocolate chip for the lady cause it's the only drink she can stand to have from here and a pistachio-coffee frappe for my boyfriend here. I'm assuming you still take the usual mocha frappe unless you're different now or whatever." I said gesturing at Ethan.

"Uh yeah that's fine, same old mocha for me."

"Great, so make that two mocha frappe and cheese scones." I said turning back to the server.

"Alright great, I'll go place your order now." she said but barely tried to move.

I sat forward as I made myself comfortable before I realized they were all looking at me.

Alejandro with a huge grin on his face and the other three like they just had the shock of their lives.

"What?"

The server was the first to respond.

"I thought the other guy was your boyfriend but hey, the two of you are fine, that's for sure. Whew child it's always the fine men that be out here loving one another. A sister be struggling in these streets."

We all started laughing uncontrollably at the randomness of what she just said. It was the perfect icebreaker to cut the tension. I'm leaving her a tip I said to myself.

"Hey I'm just saying. So, if he isn't your boyfriend does that mean he's single cause, I'm looking if you are honey." she said looking at Ethan.

We all looked at him, then he looked at Aliesha, then they both looked at me. I shrugged my shoulders, my way of saying it's whatever at this point.

"Sorry sister, but this one is all mine." Aliesha said, planting a kiss on him.

"Say less, let me get y'all those orders." She said as she walked away. "God, I see what you are doing for these fine people out in these streets, please bless me!"

We all started laughing again. The rest of the evening was filled with nothing but laughter and stories of all the stuff we missed out on. It felt great to just be there with them, I won't lie I missed them dearly.

CH. 23

Time flew by so fast that we hadn't realized three hours had already gone by.

"I missed you, I missed this." Ethan said. "I wasn't sure you'd ever forgive us or that we'd ever get move pass this. I guess we have Alejandro to thank for that."

"Ah no, I did nothing, my De might be stubborn as I'm sure as you're all way to familiar with." he said. They laughed and nodded in agreement, but I just rolled my eyes. "But the truth is, he'd already forgiven y'all.

"Really? Well maybe he should be an actor because he put on one hell of a show of hating us and shutting us out." Aliesha laughed.

Alejandro turned to me and said, "i legami forti possono essere spezzati ma sono ancora riparabili una volta che c'è amore nei tuoi cuori"

"Huh?" responded both Aliesha & Ethan.

I turned to them and said, "He says, 'Strong bonds may be broken but they're still mendable once there is love in your hearts'. It's something he taught me the pass couple of weeks."

"Oh, look at you, Mr. linguist, now, aren't you?" Ethan said punching me in the chest.

"I know a little something ha-ha."

"Well, we've got to get going, there's a movie me and Aliesha want to catch in the theatre. You're welcome to join us if you want, Ale and Deon." he said, opening his wallet.

"Oh, don't worry about the bill, I've taken care of

it already and me and De are going to stay here a little longer, I've quite grown to like this place. It has a certain charm to it."

"Alright, I know what you mean. Well take good care of him for me will you. Again, thank you for this evening." Ethan said. He turned to me and flashed a bright smile, "And Deon, you're still the greatest and sweetest person I know."

"Yeah, I know." I said in the cockiest impersonation ever.

"Bye Deon and Alejandro, it was very nice meeting you, take care of my baby boy now." Aliesha said as she got up and gave him a hug.

They were about to walk off when I remembered something.

"Wait up guys!" I shouted. They stopped and turned around. I threw myself at them and hugged them both. "I love you guys and please let's stay in touch."

I turned to go sit back down then I said with smirk on my face, "Oh Aliesha, Ethan is a pretty good kisser, super tender lips too."

She looked at me all wild eyed and then at Ethan who look to the floor as he tried to hide a blush, but she meant she had to have the last say so she hit me the best way she knows how.

"That's why I love my kisses down low, darling." she said and walked off.

I could hear Alejandro laughing behind me as he held my hand and pulled me back down next to him. What a total bitch and a diva. I really didn't need to hear that, but she just had to.

"How do you feel now De?"

"I feel pretty good, I guess you were right after all, it's just what I needed."

"I know, I'm always right si, it's hard work." He said smiling at me. "So, I'm your boyfriend now, aren't I? How were you so sure of this?"

"It was a calculated risk. You had everything to gain as I had nothing to lose. If I'm yours, you win and even if I wasn't, we're partners so technically by law, or as the contract states, I'm still yours and you're mine."

He laughed before gently kissing me on the lips. "It seems I am beaten at my own game.

What say we have another round of scones and frappes to go?"

"Sounds like a plan to me."

We made our way to the counter, while we waited on our orders to go. We left that evening and headed to Greeks Hills where I watched the sunset and enjoyed some frappes, and scones and with the man who loved me.

Thank you for reading

Frappe, Scones & The Boy I Love!

Please share your feedback on social media using our hashtags and handles: *#booksbymarcello #novelsbydeon and @deondremarcello*

If you enjoyed this book, please consider writing a review with your honest impressions on Amazon, Goodreads, or the platform of your choosing. Your feedback is incredibly valuable for helping independent authors like us to reach a wider audience.

www.ingramcontent.com/pod-product-compliance
Lightning Source LLC
Chambersburg PA
CBHW072057150726
47999CB00005B/1808